Tessa on TV

OXFORD
UNIVERSITY PRESS

"Cheer up, Tessa," said her mother. Tessa didn't want to cheer up. All she could think about was how much she would like to have a dog. But her parents said a dog would cost too much money to feed.

Tessa and her family lived on the small island of Riduna. Her mum and dad had a small Bed and Breakfast business, but there weren't many visitors to the island.

In the holidays Tessa got extra pocket money for helping in her aunt's café, but there still wasn't much money left over for a dog.

Tessa had a bit of money saved up, but it wasn't enough. The only thing she had to sell was a funny old coin her grandfather had given her.

Tessa's grandfather said that a pirate had given it to a boy in their family, but that was long, long ago. Tessa wasn't sure if it was true or a made-up story.

Tessa sighed and went off to help at the café. For once the café was quite busy. There was a big man with glasses who kept talking all the time. His name was Mr Jones. Sitting with Mr Jones were two young men and a girl who hardly said a word.

Tessa's aunt whispered to her, "They're visitors. They want to film the island for a holiday programme on television. We will all be famous!" But she laughed as she said it, so Tessa knew she was joking.

There was a van outside, full of cameras and big
metal boxes. Tessa peered at it through the window.
"What will they film?" asked Tessa, but nobody knew.

"Perhaps they'll film me," said Tessa hopefully when she told her family the news that evening. Her brother Jack was so much bigger and louder than she was, that sometimes she felt almost invisible. If she was on television, then everybody would see her!

"Why should they film you?" laughed Jack.
Tessa scowled at him.

Later, when Tessa was playing with her baby sister, she told her about the television people. The baby just blew some bubbles, then fell fast asleep.

Soon everybody on the island was talking about the television people. It was a very quiet island where everybody knew what was going on. They wondered what the film would be about.

Mr Jones, the film director, began to grumble. "Nothing much happens in this place," he said loudly. "There's nothing here for us to film. We'll have to pack up and go home at the end of the week."

The islanders were sorry to hear this. But nobody could think of anything they could do to make the island more exciting.

"Perhaps you'd better take them shrimping with you," said Tessa's father. "You might catch a sea monster!"

"Just don't go out too far. Remember it's the low tides," said her mother. "So don't get your clothes all wet when the tide turns."

But she knew they would. They always did.

Tessa and Jack walked down to the bay. Tessa kept thinking what fun it would be if they had a dog with them. Jack wondered what sort of things would interest film crews.

The sea was far, far out. This low, low tide only happened twice a year and they could see rocks and bits of old boats which were usually underwater.

They caught quite a lot of shrimps. Then Jack started to go further out looking for ormers. Ormers are fish which live inside big shells. When the shells are opened, the insides are all the colours of the rainbow.

A van stopped in the sand dunes and Tessa saw it was the television people. She waved to them and they climbed down onto the beach. Then Tessa forgot about them as she saw how far out Jack had gone. She went after him.

Jack had got a lot of ormers in his bucket. He was just looking for more, when Tessa noticed that on the other side of the rock there were some strange looking shapes sticking out of the sea.

They were all covered in seaweed, but they were the same shape as her father's old fishing boat – only bigger!

"It's an old wreck," shouted Tessa.

She and Jack stared at it, then at each other.

"Let's go and find Dad," said Jack. Their father was very interested in old wrecks.

"Perhaps the television people will give us a lift," said Jack. The pair of them splashed back to the shore.

"A wreck?" said Mr Jones, "I don't believe it. You're pulling my leg. Still, we might as well have a quick look. Bring the camera, Pete!"

As the tide was still going out, more and more of the wreck was showing. Mr Jones and Pete stared at it with their mouths open.

"There are old wrecks all round the island," said Tessa. "People have to be very careful when they go out in their boats. There were pirate boats coming in here for hundreds of years."

"Tell me all about it," said Mr Jones. "Pete, get that camera going. Stand by the wreck, Tessa. You're not very tall so you'll make the wreck look even bigger!"

The news of the wreck went round the island in a flash and in no time at all the islanders were telling their own favourite wreck story. Pete's camera was working non-stop and Mr Jones was smiling from ear to ear.

A few weeks later, Tessa was on TV. The programme made the whole island famous. People from all over the world were booking tickets to come and visit.

At home, the phone never stopped ringing.

"We're going to have a very busy year," said Tessa's dad. "The Bed and Breakfast is fully booked all summer, so there'll be enough money for you to have a dog, Tessa. Well done the pair of you!"

Tessa and Jack grinned at each other. Then Tessa went up to her room and got out her old gold coin. She wouldn't have to sell it after all. In fact, she was going to keep it for ever and ever.

And tomorrow she was going to get a dog.